Save the Bengal Tiger!

adapted by Billy Lopez
illustrated by Cassandra Berger,
Little Airplane Productions

SIMON SPOTLIGHT/NICK JR.
New York London Toronto Sydney

Based on the TV series *Wonder Pets!*™ as seen on Nick Jr.®

SIMON SPOTLIGHT
An imprint of Simon & Schuster Children's Publishing Division
1230 Avenue of the Americas, New York, New York 10020

Manufactured in the United States of America
First Edition 10 9 8 7 6 5 4 3 2 1
ISBN-13: 978-1-4169-6495-7
ISBN-10: 1-4169-6495-9

Ring, ring! The tin can rattled and shook.
The Wonder Pets leaped from their cages to look.

They picked up the phone, and guess what they saw?
A Bengal tiger with a thorn in her paw!

"Oochee! Oochee!" they heard her yelp.

So, of course, the Wonder Pets offered to help.

"Wonder Pets, let's build the Flyboat," said Linny.
But their marble was stuck in a straw that was skinny!
They tried reaching in to grab hold of it,
but all of their hands were too big to fit!

Then Ming-Ming noticed a fly passing by,
and asked him if he could give it a try.

"Great idea, Ming-Ming!" said Tuck. "After all, our
hands are too big and we need someone small!"

It worked! The Wonder Pets thanked him and flew out of the classroom and into the blue.

"Wonder Pets, Wonder Pets, we're on our way!
To help a Bengal tiger and save the day!
We're not too big and we're not too tough,
but when we work together we've got the right stuff!

GO, WONDER PETS!
YAY!"

They soared through the beautiful Indian skies
and followed the sound of the poor tiger's cries.

"Oochee! Oochee!" they could hear her shout.
"The thorn hurts, Wonder Pets, please pull it out!"

“The thorn is too small, we can’t get a grip!
Each time we try to pull it, we slip!”

The tiger was feeling sad as could be,
when suddenly in walked a mouse named Raji!

“I’m Raji, the Puller of Thorns!” he declared.
“I can pull out your thorn!” But the tiger just stared.

“You’re just a mouse, tiny and small!
Someone your size couldn’t help me at all!”

"But tiger," said Tuck. "Don't you realize?
All creatures are special, no matter what size!"
The tiger was sorry. She politely said,
"Forgive me, dear Raji, please go ahead."

So Raji tried pulling with all of his might,
but the thorn wouldn't budge, it was stuck in too tight!

“I’m sorry,” said Raji. “I should have known.
The thorn is too deep to pull out on my own.”

"Don't worry," said Linny. "I know what to do! You pull the thorn, Raji, and we'll pull you!"

"What's gonna work? TEAMWORK!

What's gonna work? TEAMWORK!"

Out came the thorn! “Our work here is done!
To the Flyboat,” said Linny. “Good-bye, everyone!”

And they all celebrated with celery . . . and curry!

"Wait," said the tiger. "What's the big hurry?"